Escape To Goma

Vuyo Ngcakani

Escape to Goma

Vuyo Ngcakani

Vuyo Ngcakani

Escape to Goma is a novel, a work of fiction, and a product of the author's imagination. Any resemblance to actual events or persons, living or dead, is entirely coincidental.

©2022

Front cover by Rebecca Payne

CONTENTS

Dedicated to my grandchildren. May they know a little bit of Africa, the continent of their grandfather.

Chapter 1 - Fleeing

"Tola, wake up. Hurry!"

Tola's mom shakes him roughly out of a deep sleep. She pulls him out of bed and hands him his baby sister.

"Take Nomsa and let's go."

"What's going on?" asks Tola, groggily.

His mom runs out of his room, his 4-year-old sister Lindi looking scared and bawling, fastened on her back. Tola follows her quickly, placing Nomsa on his hip. At twelve years old, he is the oldest and only son and is responsible for helping his mom with the girls and around the home. For the most part, he doesn't mind doing it, but sometimes he has to give up playing football with his friends or sometimes they interrupt him as he does his homework. He wishes his dad were home more.

Tola Matthews wants to make his dad proud of him. Everything he does is to that end, even doing things that he doesn't enjoy or he isn't good at, like football or intonga(stick fighting), both for which his dad is renowned in the village of Dlambona. Tola prefers reading or drawing to sport but his dad likes to see him out there in competition. He is Tola's biggest fan.

Tola practices every day so that when his dad returns to Dlambona, he will see an improvement in his skills. Dad is a domestic in the city of Lobani and returns to the village once a month. He says he makes more money working for the Bukani's than he would if he continued working the farm growing maize and spinach and selling it at the local market. Tola doesn't care about the money. He just wants his dad home.

In about a week, he will be. Before falling asleep, he had marked off October 8th, 1986, todays date, on the calendar. He is counting down the days until Dad's return. Little does he know that October 8th will be a date that he will never forget.

A shrill scream paralyzes him briefly but seeing Mom race through the hut propels him forward. He steps on something which makes him stumble. He looks back to see his pocket bible with the New Testament and Psalms that his dad had given him on his last return. He snatches it up and chases down his mom.

The village is on fire, lighting up the night. As Tola chases after his mom, he sees men setting other homes ablaze. Men lie on the ground while others are being beaten up.

The Gamba tribe.

They are a notorious, warrior nation, bent on conquering and pillaging; they kill the men and take the women and children. The village prepared for this, and had had drills, with escape routes and places to meet, should the Gamba attack them.

"Stop!" comes a command from behind him.

A bullet then whizzes by his right ear. He moves Nomsa in front of him to shield her and imagines himself playing football, dribbling through defenders, moving side to side, until he disappears into the thick bush. Nomsa wakes up and starts crying. He reaches his mom, grateful that he could still see her thanks to the fire behind them.

"Keep running," urges Mom.

They aren't the only ones on the run. Many villagers are trying to escape the ambush, running in different directions. Most run with them as the protective bushes provide cover from the ambushers.

Tola doesn't know how long they have been running but Nomsa begins to feel heavy and he doesn't know how much longer he can carry her. His legs ache; he wants to stop and rest. He looks at his mom and sees that she, too, is dragging her feet.

"We have to keep going Tola," she said. "We can't stop yet. Here, drink some water."

Tola wishes for a cool night breeze that never comes. The still air, thick with heat, is another obstacle they have to overcome. The moon is high and bright and the countless stars add their light as well.

Dlambona is long out of view. Tola wonders who has made it out, who has been taken captive, and who has been killed. There are about twenty people in their group. He knows them all as their village is small and everyone knows each other. His standard 7 teacher, Mr. Kamala, holds his two children in each arm. Surveying the group, Tola notices his wife is not with him and fears the worst.

God, keep her safe. A prayer is said just in case.

It feels like hours before they stop to rest. The first light of dawn peeks, revealing several destroyed huts. It was a village.

"What is this place, Mama?" asked Tola.

"It looks like they met the same fate we did, my son."

"Do you think it's safe to stay here? The Gamba might come back."

Mama smiles at him and then walks toward the men who have gathered and are discussing a course of action. They then spread out and go through each hut or what is left of them. As the day brightens the destruction becomes evident. Roofless, half-walled huts are all that is left of the homes. Metal pots having fallen in stomped-out fires, knocked over wooden receptacles for pounding maize, and clothes left hanging on lines were everywhere: signs that this village had been hit and abandoned. Tola notices a makeshift football field, with two sticks stuck in the ground as goalposts. Dlambona probably looks exactly like this.

"Come, Tola," his mom calls. "We will rest over here."

She points to a couple of Jacaranda trees in the midst of the destruction. Tola is amazed that they survived as the flames must have been close. They show signs of charring but still provide some shade. Some grass is gathered for the babies, while the rest sleep on the ground using rocks as pillows. Two, though exhausted, kept watch, the plan to rotate them as soon as possible.

As he always does before bed, Tola prays. *"Jesus, thank you for getting us out safely. My whole family is alive and I am grateful. Please continue to watch over us and everybody else. Thank you, Jesus. I love you. Amen."*

The sun is at its zenith when Tola awakens. Looking over his surroundings reminds him of the nightmare they are in. His sisters sleep peacefully beside him, while his mom tends to a pot nearby. She beckons him over.

"Taste this," she says.

His mom was the best cook. His friends liked to come over because his mom made the best and tastiest meals. She used him as her taste-tester and he loved it. Tola loves his mom. He can see that she is trying to remain strong, for their sake, but this ordeal has to be hard on her. He knows that he will have to be strong too, to show her that she doesn't have to worry about him; he can take care of himself.

"Delicious," he fibs. It's nothing like what she usually cooks. "When did you hunt for rabbit?"

"Liar," she says, smiling. "We brought it with us. We knew there was a possibility of the Gamba coming to our village so we had food and water put aside in case we had to leave quickly. We didn't bother with spices though, just salt."

She stirs the broth some more. She looks worn out. She catches Tola looking at her and seeks to reassure him. "We're going to be fine, Tola. We're going to see your dad in Lobani. The people he works for are very nice and will let us stay in the servant's quarters for a while. Don't worry. Everything is going to work out. We're in Jesus' hands, right?"

Tola nodded. "Are we going back to our village again?"

"I don't know, Tola, I truly don't know."

Tola sees her eyes well up. As he hugs her, Nomsa starts crying waking up Lindi as well. Mom quickly eats then nurses Nomsa as the others feed themselves.

"How long will it take to reach Lobani?" asked Tola.

"There is a bus that leaves Goma tonight. We are going to try to make that. We should be in Lobani by morning."

"Tata will be surprised to see us."

Mr. Kamala approaches them. "Jalisa, you should start walking if you're going to catch the Lobani bus. Hello, Master Matthews. How are you doing?"

"I'm doing fine, Mr. Kamala," replies Tola. His teacher calls his students by their last names.

"Good. Your mother needs you to be strong, to help her with your sisters. Can you do that?"

"Yes, sir. Aren't you coming with us?"

Mr. Kamala shakes his head. "I'm going back to find my wife. I need to know if she is still alive."

As they depart, Tola notices that many others stay behind. They are the only ones leaving.

"They are all staying to return to look for their loved ones," says his mom. "They are hopeful but the truth is many of them will be looking for dead people."

Tola thinks of the friends he probably will never see again. He feels guilty that in the rush to flee, he hasn't given them much thought. Some of them may be dead or recruited into the Gamba militia. He has heard of cases where the boys are told to shoot their family members, given drugs, and brainwashed.

Tola quickly reads his favourite Psalm which is number 23. He thinks of Jesus as their shepherd, guiding them to Goma, being with them through any evil they may encounter, and comforting them with his rod and staff. He grabs the two goalpost sticks as they passed them on their way.

Chapter 2 - Fighting

Thankfully Mom knows the way as she has made the trip a few times. Tola has only been to Lobani once and can't remember how to get there or to Goma. Mom moves quickly with Nomsa on her back. Tola and Lindi walk most of the time with Nomsa switching to Tola when Lindi is carried by Mom.

They stay off paths and dusty roads, wanting to stay away from a possible ambush from bandits. With no men travelling with them, they would be vulnerable to attack from those who would see them as weak. The cloudless sky allows the sun's rays to unleash their heat on the travellers. Mom carries just enough water to get them to Goma, not wanting to load them down with extra weight. They would replenish their rations in Goma.

"We're halfway there," says Mom as they sit down to rest. Looking at the sun she continues, "I think we can get there before it gets dark but we have to walk faster. Just a little bit."

She adds clarification when she sees the look on Tola's face.

"You're my little man," she says, rubbing his head. "I'm glad you're here helping me with the girls. I couldn't have asked for a better son."

Tola's reaction to his mom's compliment surprised him. His eyes moistened as he stood up.

"What are we waiting for?" he quips, energized. "Let's go."

"Yes, let's go," echoed Lindi.

Her outburst brought a laugh from all of them. She hadn't said anything the whole journey so far, so her words were a pleasant surprise. Even Nomsa looked like she had a smile on her face. Actually, her smile had nothing to do with Lindi. "I'm going to change Nomsa and then we can be on our way."

Nomsa laughs as she is being changed. *It's good that a 6-month-old has no idea what they face*, thinks Tola. With all of them enthralled with her, no one notices a man sneak into their presence. It was Lindi who saw him first and screams.

Though startled, Mom remains calm and continues to change her baby.

"Hello," she greets.

Tola notices that the man has a machete with what looks like it has dried blood on it. He knows that from the goats, chickens, and other livestock he has assisted in slaughtering. He doesn't like the look in the man's eyes and he clutches the goal sticks a little tighter, grateful that he has them.

"My name is Jalisa and these are my children Tola, Lindi, and Nomsa."

The man stares at Jalisa. He looks her up and down then steps forward. She moves her children behind her as they match his forward progress with their backward movement. He rushes forward. Mom falls backwards as she moves too quickly and trips over Lindi causing her to fall as well. Mom drops hard as she fights to keep Nomsa from hitting the ground. As the man closes in, Tola steps up and stands between the man and his mom.

"Tola, get back!" orders Mom.

Tola doesn't listen. "Mom, get up and move back," he orders, as he holds the two sticks in front of him.

"Tola!"

"No! Move back!"

There must have been something in Tola's voice because Mom obeys. The man sneers, not thinking much of his opponent. One thing Dad taught him was to never underestimate your adversary. Generally, if they are smaller than you, then they have the advantage of speed and agility. If they are bigger than you, as this man was, they have the advantage of strength. Know whom you are facing, and fight accordingly.

The man brandishes his machete.

"Why don't you leave us alone?" Tola says, hoping to reason with the man. "Our village was attacked by the Gamba and burnt down. All our possessions are gone. We are on our way to see my Dad and we can't miss the bus in Goma. Please let us be on our way."

The man rushes him. Tola remembers his training and as the man swings his weapon, Tola ducks and sticks his leg out. The man stumbles and falls, grass pricking his eyes and getting into his mouth. Tola moves making sure he is always between the man and his family.

The man points the machete at Tola and rushes again. Tola is grateful that the man is slow and skirts him making sure he keeps him moving. It doesn't take long for the man to start panting and slowing down. He makes one last rush. As he raises the machete, Tola whacks his wrist. The machete flies out of his hand. Tola strikes the side of his neck, felling him to his knees. He hits his Adams apple and the man topples like a baobab tree.

Tola stands over his victim. *Now I understand how David felt when he slew Goliath,* he thought. He has no desire to remove the man's head though. His Mom's call wakes him from his euphoric reflection.

"Tola! Let's go!"

He backs away from the man and joins his mom and sisters. They rush from the scene, looking back occasionally to ensure that they are not being pursued.

"Mom, I'm thirsty," announces Lindi.

Mom realises in their haste they left their rations at the last resting place. She looks at the sun and sees that they still have enough daylight left that the heat could be a problem, but she doesn't want to stop as they had lost some time when the man appeared.

"Let's keep going," she says, looking at Tola to keep him from saying anything regarding their food and water supply. "We'll rest again soon."

Tola takes Nomsa from her and she carries Lindi. "Close your eyes and rest, little one," she coaxes. She hums Lindi's favourite lullaby.

"Are we almost there, Mama?" asks Tola.

"It's a while yet, my son. But we will be there before it gets dark. We are doing well."

That is said for Lindi's benefit. Tola knows better. *Lord, please help us.* He is thirsty as well and Nomsa taxes his back.

"I see a Jackalberry tree in the distance. I could go and pick us some fruit."

He thinks that it's a mirage at first but Mom's response confirms its existence.

"No, Tola. That tree is way off course and will just delay us further. We will be fine until we get to Goma." She looks at him approvingly, and adds, "I am so proud of you."

That is the second compliment Mama has given him. Tola had always sought Tata's approval and never gave much thought to the praise of his mama. Today, for the first time he realises its value and how much he needs it.

Lindi starts to cry. Mama looks at her and notices that she's lethargic. She feels warm to the touch. Mama tries to get her to suck on her breast. Lindi resists.

"Come on, Lindi," she insists. "You need to eat something."

"This is Nomsa's food," says Lindi weakly.

"There's enough for both of you. Please, Lindi."

But Lindi would have none of it. Tola tries to help convince her but she doesn't budge.

"Mama, we're wasting time. That tree is our only chance right now."

Jalisa sighs knowing that Tola is right.

"You keep walking so we don't lose too much time," says Tola firmly. He takes off his sweat-soaked shirt and ties it to one of the goal sticks. "Every so often lift this up so I know where you are. I know we are moving away from the sun so I will know where to look. Hold it up briefly then put it down. We don't need others to see your position."

"Be careful," pleads Mama. "We need you."

"I will."

Tola starts in a slow jog. He could go faster but because he hasn't had water or food, he doesn't want to waste energy. Slow and steady Tata always said. If he could see him now. He can't wait to tell him about the events of today, especially how he protected his wife and daughters. He will be so proud.

The presence of the Jackalberry tree means that there will be animals nearby. The fruit and leaves of the tree are enjoyed by many species including giraffes, rhinos, baboons, kudu, buffalo, and warthogs. The animals that eat of the Jackalberry tree aren't the ones that Tola is worried about. He is concerned about the carnivores that eat the Jackalberry-loving beasts. Lions and hyenas, which travel in packs, are especially worrisome.

Mama and his sisters are on the move as noted by the displaced raised flag. Surveying the scene surrounding the tree, giraffes are easy to spot. Besides some birds, he doesn't see any other animals. *Things are not always what they seem,* thinks Tola, reciting another of Tata's teachings. He proceeds cautiously, his stick ready to use if necessary.

As he nears the tree, the giraffes slowly gait away. This gives Tola some confidence and he moves a little quicker. He wants to be gone before other animals show up. Much to his disappointment, there is no fruit on the ground around the tree. Jackalberry trees are easy to climb, but he had hoped he wouldn't have to do so. Leaping up, he grabs onto the lowest branch and swings up to scale the tree.

As he ascends, he notices that the giraffes have depleted much of the fruit. He just needs two or three fruit to take to his family. He sees one branch that has the fruit he needs and notices why the giraffe may have passed it by. Hanging off it was a hive of African bees.

Tola is grateful for the time of day it is for the late afternoon is when the bees start to settle down. One or two buzzes near the hive, but the activity is light. He reaches out to knock the fruit down with his stick but is not close enough. Thankful for the sturdy branch, he inches closer to the fruit and hence also the hive. A couple more bees exit their home, daring him to edge closer.

He whacks lightly on the fruit. It swings but doesn't release. He strikes the fruit harder to no avail. A bee approaches him and buzzes around his head. He lies still. Moments later, it flies away. Tola crawls closer to get better leverage. He smacks the fruit again but it is stuck fast. He knows he is going to have to pluck the fruit by hand.

A family of warthogs wanders nearby. It is probably a good thing the fruit didn't fall because the pigs would have eaten them before he got down. From the tree, he sees the flag marking the progress of his family. Mama is moving quite fast considering her load. She must trust that he would be quick, but neither of them anticipated this problem of having to climb the tree and face bees.

Jesus, please help me.

The warthogs are under the tree, looking for something to eat. A crazy idea pops into Tola's mind. It is his one chance for success. He edges closer to the hive and readies his stick.

Whack! Whack!

Two quick strikes fells the hive down onto the path of the warthogs, who are sent fleeing as the bees attack. Tola quickly harvests the fruit and before he descends the tree, he surveys the horizon.

"Come on, come on," he mutters, urging Mama to lift the flag. Glancing down at the hive he sees bees buzzing around their fallen home. Moments later he spots the flag.

He scrambles down the tree and jogs off in pursuit of his family. A glance back secures in his mind that the bees have other priorities.

He feels proud of himself that he had the flag idea. It works like a charm as in less than half-an-hour he meets up with his family. They have stopped for a rest as Mama found carrying both girls tiring. Lindi was lethargic and limp. Mama squeezes some fruit juice into her mouth. She then gives her some fruit to chew on.

"Let's go," she says. "We still have time to make it but we have to hurry. Take Nomsa."

"I can carry Lindi, Mama," says Tola.

Jalisa smiles. "My little man," she says proudly. "I know you can, my son. I want to take Lindi so I can keep an eye on her. That's all."

They share a piece of fruit as they continue their journey. Tola is grateful for his Mama's wisdom as he starts to feel tired. Thankfully Nomsa has stayed asleep. He looks over at Lindi who gives him a weary smile. He smiles back, pleased that she looks much better.

Tola can tell they are almost there by the increase in people they pass, probably going to get water, or heading back to their village after having bought goods at the market. Whatever the reason, realizing that they were just a bus ride away from seeing Tata, puts a skip in his step.

"Where's the bus stop, Mama?" he asks.

"Straight ahead, where those people are waiting."

As they approach the stop, the bus rolls up. Many disembark while others hustle to go onboard. They join the crowd and inch toward the door. As they get close the driver sees them.

"Hey," he yells. "Can't you see the lady has three children? Let her through."

The people oblige and others inside give them their seats so they can sit together, Lindi on Mama's lap and Nomsa in Tola's arms. He leans her on his chest to relieve the weight on his arms. It is a long trip to Lobani.

As the bus pulls out, Tola looks behind him, knowing that moment by moment, more distance is added between himself and his village. *Oh Dlambona, will I ever see you again.* Sadness overwhelms him and he is unable to control his tears. The events of the day have worn his twelve-year-old body out, and he just wants to be playing football or intonga or reading his favourite book. He leans against his Mama and weeps. She says nothing. She kisses him and just lets him cry.

Chapter 3 - Forgetting

The bus ride to Lobani is broken up into three sections. That's what Tola's dad told him. There is the dirt road section, the gravel road section, and the tarred road section. At the end of each section is a town where the bus stops to refuel and allow passengers a bathroom break, some food and to stretch. Of the twelve-hour trip, six is a dirt road that ends in Nakuru. The next is gravel which ends in Dembe. It takes four hours. The tarred road makes its way into Lobani.

Tola looks out into the night. They are on the outskirts of Goma and the streetlights come to an end and the savannah grasslands begin. It is difficult to see the thick tall grass with shrubs and small trees scattered along either side of the road but they are there. The bus chugs along, picking up speed slowly. It is loud but the shocks must have been new because the ride isn't too bumpy. The compartment has ten rows of seats on either side that fit two adults per seat. Tola ends up at the window with Lindi in the middle and Mom carries Nomsa on the aisle. They are close to the back.

The night is dark. Now that they have left the bright lights of the city, they are at the mercy of the moon and the stars. They are ineffective because of the cloud cover which has moved in fast. It would have been nice if the arrival had been reversed, with cloud in the day and clear skies at night. Oh to be like Jesus, who controls the wind and the waves.

"Try to get some sleep, Tola," says Mama. "It's a long ride and you don't know when you'll get another opportunity."

Tola nods his agreement, leans back, and closes his eyes. A while later, he isn't sure how long, he opens them up again. He is the only one on the seat. He looks to the back where the bathroom is and sees that the whole bus is empty. He turns to get the bus driver's attention and is horrified to see that the bus is driving itself. He can't breathe, his heart races, his brow moistens, and after a lot of effort he calls out, "Maaaaaaa!"

"Tola!" Mama gently shakes him. "Tola!"

Tola awakens startled and slightly disoriented.

"You were having a nightmare, my son. Everything is fine."

Tola takes a couple of deep breaths. He had probably stopped breathing for real. Relief rolls over him like a fast-moving wave. He can feel his heart's rhythmic thudding. He is never so happy to see his family, a bus full of passengers, and a driver. He gives Lindi a big hug.

"How long was I asleep?"

"A couple of hours," Mama says. "I have to change Nomsa. We'll be right back"

Tola watches as his mom makes her way to the bathroom. He smiles at Lindi as she cuddles into him. Someone gets up from the front of the bus and makes their way toward them. The bus is dimly lit so it isn't until he walks past them that Tola sees who it was. It was the man he fought on the way to Goma. The man doesn't glance down at them so Tola has no idea if he had seen them. The man stands outside the bathroom as if he is waiting for Mama to come out and there is no way for Tola to warn her.

So he watches. He doesn't have the intonga sticks with him. He left them in the luggage compartment under the bus. Mama comes out carrying his baby sister and she bumps right into the man. Tola sees her eyes widen as she recognizes him. The man leans in and says something to her. Then he steps aside and lets her pass. She hurries over and sits down clearly shaken.

"What did he say to you, Mama," asks Tola.

Mama just shakes her head but doesn't speak. Her sheepish smile fails to reassure him. It angers him to see her like this.

"Let's switch spots," he says, getting up.

He doesn't wait for a response. He wouldn't have taken no for an answer. If Mama had refused he would have stood in the aisle. Mama doesn't refuse, probably because it would be safer for Nomsa and Lindi. She is also too tired to argue.

"Mama, try to get some sleep," begs Tola. "It's unlikely that the man will do anything. We are in a bus full of people."

Mama wraps a blanket around her and ties it off at the shoulder making a mini hammock for Nomsa. Lindi stretches across the seat, her head on Mom's lap and her legs over Tola. It doesn't take long for them to reach lalaland, Mama with one eye open.

Tola faces forward anticipating the opening of the bathroom door. The hinges squeaked vund his heart rate picked up. He wishes he had chameleon eyes so that he could see the man approaching. The human hearing would have to do. He contemplates turning to face the man, to have their eyes meet, to remind the man who he's up against. But he doesn't. The man closes in and as he passes, he smacks the back of Tola's head. Tola glares. The man sneers and continues to his seat.

Then it starts to rain.

The windshield wipers are frantic, squeegeeing the downpour aside. To Tola, it looks fruitless. The driver has slowed down to a sloth pace. Tola would have pulled over and waited the torrent out. His sisters don't stir at all but even though she tries to hide it, Mom looks concerned. She smiles at him but says nothing.

They are halfway to Nakuru. While it took about three hours to get to this point, it will probably take four to get to the town. They still have some fruit from the Jackalberry tree which Tola partakes off. Lindi will need some when she wakes up.

He sees it before the driver does. Is the driver sleeping? The headlights light up a family of ostriches as they race across the street.

"Look out!"

There is a beat before the bus swerves right. It hits the trailing ostrich sending it higher than it ever thought possible. The bus swings left to avoid slamming into a tree only to face the possibility of crashing into another. The slippery, wet and now muddy road makes it challenging to straighten and control the vehicle.

Mama is screaming. She isn't the only one but she is the only one that Tola hears. At Tola's initial "look out" yell she had grabbed all three of her children and covered them like a hen covers her chicks. Tola clutches the headrest on the seat in front of them to try and lessen the bouncing back and forth that they are experiencing. As the bus swings right again the centrifugal force tosses him into the nearby seat occupants like a merry-go-round would anyone who let go of the bars. He knocks his head against the window and his mom's screams fade as he blacks out.

5-year-old Tola waved to his dad. Tata smiled and waved back. Tola was so happy that Tata made it home to watch his football game. Because he was the goalie he had time to frequently glance over and wave. So he did. Except that, on this occasion, the opponent closed in and kicked the ball which bounced off his head knocking him out cold.

"Tola! Tola!" A man's voice calls out to him and also lightly slaps at his face. As Tola comes to, he thinks he is hearing his dad's voice. But as the cobwebs clear he sees that it was the man he fought. He tries to back up but as he sits up his head swims and he has to lie down again.

"Don't try to get up, son," says the man, maliciously. "Tata's here. I'll look after you."

He presses down on Tola's chest preventing him from moving. He needn't have bothered. Tola wasn't going anywhere. His heart thunders, his head throbs, and he loses consciousness again.

The centrifugal force also knocks Mama into the adjacent seat but her fall is broken by the passenger she falls into. Their heads bounce off each other like bowling ball-sized billiard balls. As only a mother could, she holds onto her children as she is knocked around getting groggier with each bounce. Miraculously, the driver gains control of the bus and pulls over to the side of the road to assess damages to the passengers and the bus. Mama is thankful that the children are wailing because it means that they are alive. Adrenaline shoots through her as she checks them over. No blood. No goose-eggs. They cling to her and she clings to them. She gives thanks to God that her children have survived the incident. She looks around and sees a young boy lying unconscious on the bus floor. He looks familiar, really familiar but she doesn't know why. A familiar man comes over to look after him so she doesn't think anything more of it.

Nakuru is the nearest town with a hospital so it is deemed best that the journey continues. The rain continues to teem down. There is no damage to the bus but there are a few passengers who need medical care.

Tola is one of them. The man brings Tola to his seat to be with him. No one questions him. Some show concern for Tola and offer to assist in any way they can. He declines any aid and props Tola up by the window, making him look like he is asleep.

It is around 1 am when Tola comes around. He is facing the window as he awakens so he sees the reflection of the man. The man turns to face him so Tola pretends to still be unconscious. It is all he can do to control his breathing. He recalls the accident with the ostrich, the bus losing control and being hurled into the adjacent seat. That is it. Seeing the man briefly must have been a dream. Now it is reality as he sits next to him. Where are Mama and the girls? Something must be wrong. There is no way that he would be sitting with this man unless something has happened to Mama. Is she still on the bus?

The bus crawls into Nakuru around 4 am and makes its way to the hospital. As it slows to a stop Tola springs off his seat surprising the man. He manages to elude the man's grasp and race to the back where Mama and his sisters are.

"Mama!"

He doesn't get the reaction he expects. Mama is startled and backs away in her seat drawing his sisters to her. Is he dreaming again?

"Tola," said Lindi.

That was promising.

"Mama? Are you okay? It's me, Tola."

The answer he got was being yanked away and led to the door. He turns and looks perplexed at his Mama. What is going on? Lindi is crying and saying his name continuously. Tola struggles to release himself from the man's vice-like grasp to no avail. He tries to punch the mans testicles. Tata said in desperate times, go for the balls. He misses. He kicks the man's shins which made him angry. The man slaps him causing his ears to ring and the earth to swirl. People watch but no one intervenes.

Mama watches. Confused. Who is this boy? There is something familiar about him and Lindi isn't afraid of him. Is he a nephew or a friend's son? He keeps looking back at her and trying to get away from that man.

"Where's Tola going, Mama?" asks Lindi, crying.

"I don't know my daughter, but I'm going to find out."

Everyone gets off the bus. She flips Nomsa on her back and secures her with a blanket. Mama and Lindi walk off the bus just in time to see Tola stumble into the hospital.

"What do you want with me?" asks Tola.

The man doesn't answer. He stops by a payphone and makes a call. He speaks a language that Tola doesn't understand. Then they make their way down a couple of hallways and toward a door with an exit sign above it. It leads to the back parking lot where a car probably awaits them. Tola tries to escape but the grip constricts like a boa does its prey.

"What do you want with me?" Tola tries again.

The man answers this time. "You will make a fine addition to our army."

Tola's blood chills. "Your army?"

The man smiles showing his fluorosis-browned teeth. "You have good combat instincts. Someone like you will be good for our boys."

Both his parents had told him stories about these boy soldiers, how they are taken from their families, drugged, and turned into killing machines. That was something the Gamba were famous for doing. They are close to the backdoor when Tola spots a fire alarm. He knows what it was because the sign above it says 'Pull in case of Fire.' He pulls it.

Mama stays by the entrance watching the man make his phone call. As they walk off she follows making sure she stays well back. She puts her index finger to her lips, gesturing Lindi to be quiet. She makes sure that they are never in the hallway at the same time. She stays at the corner, watching which direction they turn then rushes up to the next corner so as not to miss the next turn. They veer left down the last hallway. Mama peeks round the bend just in time to see Tola pull the alarm.

The bell is situated right above her so her ears receive the full effect of its clangour. She can feel her eardrums vibrate. The din reminds her of the last time she heard the clanging of a bell which was when they had to flee from their homeland a couple of days ago. She recalls that night as the fire blazed around them, collecting her daughters and awakening her son and making a run… her son!

Both her daughters were wailing having been startled by the fire bell. A couple of men in scrubs come out of a room behind her and started heading in the opposite direction toward the front entrance.

"Help! Help!" she screams.

They rush toward her and she hands her children to them. Without an explanation, she rushes down the hall, through the door that the man had dragged Tola through, and emerges just in time to see a car drive up, no doubt to whisk Tola away. She wasn't having it.

The bell cry was drowned out by the roar only a mother could make. Without slowing down, her hands came up, nails exposed like a cheetah readying to impale her prey. The man's face was her target and with her howl having paralyzed him, he didn't stand a chance.

Her nails dig in like a scalpel to flesh. Her fingers track down from his eyes to his chin. His roar of pain join the noise as he cast Tola aside. He pushed Mama away from him as the men in scrubs burst onto the scene with Nomsa and Lindi. Seeing them, the man jumps into the car commanding the driver to go.

"Are you okay, my son?" asks Mama.

Tola just embraces his Mama, thankful that she is back.

"Madam, let's go back inside," says one of the men in scrubs. He introduces himself as Joe Mwangi. "We shouldn't be out here in the rain."

The bell stops suddenly and the atmosphere is eerily still. The rain is lighter than before and the bus has to continue on its journey. Some passengers stay behind for treatment and will continue their trip in two days when the next bus arrived.

"Can I make a phone call?" Mama asks.

"You can use the payphone in the hall," says Joe.

"I don't have any money," says Mama. "We had to leave our village in a hurry and on the way to Goma we were attacked and lost our belongings."

"Where are you going, Madam," asks Joe.

"My husband works in Lobani. He doesn't know that we are on our way so I would like to reach him."

Joe lets her use his office to make the call. She tried a couple of times but no one picks up.

"Madam, you all look tired and hungry. You could probably use a shower as well. My shift is over. Please come to my house and have my wife and me look after you for a while. I have to go to Lobani the day after tomorrow to pick up some supplies for the hospital. We can travel together then. Please."

Joe's impassioned plea does not fall on deaf ears. Mama looks over at Tola who hopes that his blank stare tells her to agree to Joe's offer. He is tired, sore, and desperate for a bath. She agrees to his terms.

"Thank you, madam," says Joe, smiling. "First, let me examine you and the children. We want to make sure that there are no hidden injuries."

Mama agrees. "My name is Jalisa and these are my children, Tola, Lindi, and Nomsa."

With a clean bill of health, they spend the next couple of days with Joe and his wife, Zawadi. The first day is spent cleaning up and getting a lot of sleep. Then Zawadi takes them shopping for shoes and clothes. She also buys a doll for Lindi and a football for Tola. They try calling Tata again but are unable to reach him.

"I'm really concerned," says Mama, as they set out for Lobani.

Zawadi does not accompany them. Tola sits in the front while Mama is with the girls in the back.

"Don't worry, Jalisa," says Joe. "I'm sure there's a perfectly good reason for this. Maybe the family is away on holidays and your husband is with them."

Unlikely, Mama thinks. Whenever the family went on vacation, Tata used that opportunity to come home.

"Mama, do you think we should go back to Dlambona?" asks Tola, who was thinking the same thing.

"No, my son. We're closer to Lobani so let's continue. I'm sure Joe is right that there is a perfectly good explanation for being unable to reach him."

Tola is not reassured. As he looks out the window, he marvels that just two nights ago they were in a torrential downpour and now the blue cloudless sky is before them. The 9 am sun shines brightly and warmly. It looks like a good, promising day. In a couple of hours, they will be with Tata. He looks back at Mama and they exchange smiles. Lindi and Nomsa exchange smiles with him as well. He takes a deep breath and sinks back into his seat.

Yes, everything is going to be just fine.

Chapter 4 – Finding

As they near the town of Dembe, Joe asks if anyone needs to stop for a bathroom break. The drive that would have taken four hours by bus takes them just over two hours. They are about an hour out of Lobani and Mama just wants to get there to see her husband and figure out what to do next. So does Tola. It has been about three weeks since they last saw Tata and he looks forward to being a full family again. Unfortunately, Joe needs to use the toilet so they stop.

"They have some potato chips and peanuts in the kiosk," says Joe. "Please go and get some and I'll pay when I return."

Jalisa declines the offer. "You are very kind, Joe. We don't want to take advantage of your generosity."

"Nonsense, Jalisa. Please take your children and get them a snack. I insist."

He takes off quickly before she can respond. Looking at her children she sees Tola and Lindi gazing at her expectantly.

"Okay," she says smiling. "You can pick either chips or peanuts, not both. Wait for Uncle Joe to pay for them before you take them."

The kiosk is in plain sight so Jalisa lets Tola go with Lindi for their treats. They run off gleefully and pick through the different flavours. Tola picks the salt and vinegar flavoured chips because that is his favourite. Tata always brought him a bag when he returned home. It was his favourite too. Lindi picks the ketchup flavour.

"Why don't you get the peanuts," says Tola. "That way we can share and have both treats."

Lindi agrees. As he looks around Tola observes that Dembe is a small but bustling town. It looks more like an outpost where people come to sell their crops or handmade jewelry and sculptures. There is a lot of commerce going on so Dembe is certainly an important meeting place. There is rural folk with donkey carts and traditional dress along with city folk with Audis and suits. Tata had not spoken about Dembe much as he was always just passing through.

He sees Joe coming out of the toilet building with another man that he doesn't recognize. Joe must have met someone he knew, he thinks. He waves to get Joe's attention but Joe either ignores him or doesn't see him because he heads straight for the car. His friend continues to a car that was parked a few spots beside theirs. It is a beige Peugeot 504. It looks like the car that tried to abduct him a few days before in Nakuru.

"Tola, we have to go," yells Joe.

Tola grabs Lindi and brings her to the car. They are barely in when Joe peels off and burns rubber out of the parking lot.

Jalisa is not impressed especially since Lindi is crying. "Joe, we have children in the car. What is going on?"

Joe says nothing.

Jalisa presses. "You insist that the children pick a snack and then you take back your offer without explanation."

Tola joins in. "Does this have anything to do with the man I saw you come out of the building with?"

Joe says nothing but his breathing noticeably deepens and quickens.

Tola continues. "I noticed that the car looked just like the one that I almost got thrown into in Nakuru."

Jalisa gasps.

"Look," says Joe. "I promised that I would drive you to Lobani so I will." He glances at Tola. "That model is very popular in these parts. You will see many more in Lobani. I know the experience you had must have been traumatic but try not to read into something that isn't there."

Tola isn't convinced. Unfortunately, he didn't get a look at the man that was driving the car but the whole thing made him uneasy. Something happened to change Joe's demeanor and it had to do with them. He was convinced of that.

The traffic starts getting heavier as they near Lobani. Joe has a map of the city and knows exactly where to go. The house isn't hard to find as it is just on the outskirts of the downtown area. They drive up to the address and see that it is gated and guarded.

"Well, here you are," says Joe. "I can't stay any longer. I have to pick up my supplies and go back home. Good luck."

After saying their thanks and goodbyes Tola and his family approach the gate. It has two light green rusted iron gates with arrows jutting out the top. They are attached to thick cement posts which are the ends of a thick cement wall that surrounded what looked like twelve homes Tola counted. Big homes. Tata had described them but didn't do them justice.

Mama speaks to the guards. "Hello. My name is Jalisa and these are my children. We are here to see my husband. He works for the Bukani's."

The guard beams. "Jalisa, Tola, Lindi, and Nomsa," he says as he points to each one. "My name is Cyril. Thabo has spoken about you many times. I have to let the homeowners know that they have visitors coming."

He picks up the phone and dials. After listening he says, "I'll send them up."

"The Bukanis live in house 12."

House 12 was at the far end of the estate. As they approach the front door someone steps out to meet them. Tola recognises Mrs. Bukani. Her beige blouse is neatly pressed and her navy skirt and jacket look like they had just returned from the cleaners. Tola feels like he has to shade his eyes from the glare of her shiny, black Lady Di's.

"Jalisa, kids, please come in."

Tola and Lindi glance at each other, showing their appreciation for the Bukani home. You could play football in this house, Tola thinks. She leads them through one big room that was at least 5 times the size of their whole house in Dlamboma. The second room is even larger with large, plush couches. She asks them to sit and the kids wait for Mama to find her spot before joining her there. A domestic worker comes in.

"Can you please make some sandwiches, Edna, and bring some juice. Thank you."

"Madam, we don't want to impose on you. Can we let Thabo know that we are here and we will wait for him in his quarters?" Jalisa was never one to waste time.

Mrs. Bukani looks puzzled. "Jalisa, Thabo hasn't worked for us for six months. I have no idea where he is."

Tola thinks that she must be kidding and waits for Tata to jump out from somewhere to surprise them. He was fond of playing pranks on them. He looks around the room in anticipation. Nothing happens.

"I don't understand," his Mama is saying. "He gave us no indication that he had switched jobs. We just saw him three weeks ago."

"And he told me that he still enjoys working here," adds Tola. "Mama, what's happened to Tata?"

His query is raised in a shrill tone. He clutches onto his mama's arm in an attempt to still his uncontrollably shaking hands. Has Tata been kidnapped? Has he been beaten somewhere and is dying in a ditch? Is he already dead?

Mama winces as she releases herself and draws him in. "There's got to be a reasonable explanation, Tola."

Her heart drums in her chest and she swallows to keep her dry throat from choking her. Lindi is crying as she senses that something is wrong. Nomsa sleeps through it all. Edna comes in with refreshments.

"Please eat something," begs Mrs. Bukani, to no avail.

The family was inconsolable. Mama tried to be strong but her children's pain was too much and the tears fell. She doesn't know what they are going to do next.

"Jalisa, you are welcome to stay here for a while," Mrs. Bukani says as if sensing Jalisa's dilemma. "Edna will show you to Thabo's old quarters. Take the sandwiches with you. Clearly, this has been quite a shock. We can talk later."

Edna leads them out through the back entrance, down a paved path, and to a small building. The first room is the community bathroom which has a shower stall and a couple of toilets. There is no bathtub.

The next three rooms are servants' quarters which are one-room bachelor pads. Edna is in one, Cyril the other, and Tata was in the one they entered. Everything is in four boxes.

"Cyril and I packed everything," Edna reveals. "The Bukani's kept everything for as long as they could expecting Thabo to return. He left without an explanation; that was not like him. I never knew a man with so much integrity."

Tola beams. People always speak so highly of Tata which is a blessing and a curse. It isn't easy to live up to his standards and the comparison is readily made by other adults. One thing that Tata has always said to him was that he should live his own life and find his path. He wished other people would have the same sentiments.

"You mean he didn't even say anything to you or Cyril," Mama asks.

"Not a word," Edna says. "One day he was here and the next he was not. Look, eat your sandwiches and get some rest. We'll talk some more later."

Jalisa sits down on one of the two twin beds and Tola and Lindi sit on either side of her. She offers the plate of sandwiches to them and then places it on the side table without taking any for herself. Her eyes fall on the boxes and stay there for a long time. Then she gets up and starts opening them.

The first one has shoes and jackets. Jalisa lifts out the jackets and goes through the pockets but finds nothing but pocket lint. The next box has shirts and trousers. The search there proves fruitless as well. Tola sees what she is doing and opens the third box. It has envelopes and documents. The fourth box has novels and other educational books like accounting or computing. They cast that box aside and after feeding Nomsa, and giving Lindi some paper and a pencil that they found, they start going through the contents of the third box.

They made piles of similar topics and ended up with family letters, government documents, bible study notes, and miscellaneous.

"This is strange," says Tola, as he handed his mama an envelope. It was in his Tata's handwriting and was addressed to his wife. "For some reason Tata never mailed it."

Mama's hands shake as she takes it from her son. As she opens it, Tola finds two more letters just like it, all addressed to Mama. She takes the three letters and places them in chronological order and begins reading. The first one was dated February 19, 1986. 10 months ago.

My dearest Jali, (she smiles)
I'm so sorry that you are reading this letter because it means that something must have happened to me. Either you are reading this at home in Dlambona because my belongings were shipped to you, or you are in my quarters because you came looking for me.

Jalisa considers reading the letters to herself to keep Tola from what might be coming. As she looks at her son, she reconsiders. He has shown himself to be very mature and capable during these harrowing days and she will need to rely on him going forward. He should have all the information he needs.

I'm not sure what I've got myself into. I don't want to tell you too much except to say that I was approached by a man who asked me to do a task. His name was Mr. Edgar Wanjiru. He is a friend of the Bukani's. At least that is what I thought.
Edgar actually works for the Intelligence Service and he wants me to spy on the Bukani's. They are especially interested in Mrs. Bukani. They haven't told me exactly what they are looking for. They just want me to tell them who comes by and anything suspicious. They will pay me for my involvement.
I said yes. Hopefully, this is a simple task. The Bukani's have been good to us so I hope they are innocent of whatever illegal activity the Service thinks they are doing.

I'm a little nervous. That's why I decided to write this note. I will write more should I feel the need. Edgar said they only need me for a few months.

I'm sorry that I didn't tell you about this. Please forgive me. I don't know what else to say. Sorry.

Jalisa is shocked and perplexed.

"What does it all mean, Mama?" asks Tola.

"I don't know, son," she answers as she opens the next letter. This one is dated May 31, 1986.

My dearest Jali,

It was good to see you and the kids last week. Lindi is growing so fast and our son is a little man now. I almost told you about my side job. I hate keeping things from you. You know that is not my way.

If you are at the Bukani's please be careful. I caught Edna looking for something in my room. She said she entered the wrong room but I don't believe her. I wouldn't be surprised if Wanjiru had approached her and Cyril as well. I haven't discussed this with either of them.

Wanjiru is getting impatient. I haven't found anything suspicious about the Bukanis. He refuses to tell me what they are looking for and now he wants me to search their belongings and keep an eye on their mail. I don't like it at all but the money will allow me to come home for good. That's the reason I'm doing this. I'll be careful.

Jalisa cast that letter aside and ripped opened the last one. When she found Thabo she was going to give him a piece of her mind. He was going to wish he stayed missing.

This one is dated July 4, 1986.

My dearest Jali,

As you probably now know, I no longer work for the Bukanis. Wanjiru has asked me to do something else for them. I don't want to discuss it here in case someone finds these letters. Someday I'll tell you everything.

I never found anything about the Bukanis that was nefarious. I think Wanjiru has Cyril and Edna to do his dirty work for him. They're not going to find anything. The Bukanis' are good people. You can trust them.

I'm not writing any more letters, Jali. If you are in Dlambona don't come looking for me. I'll be home soon and I'll explain what I can. If you are at the Bukanis, please leave immediately. Please, Jalisa. Don't be stubborn and listen to me.

I will see you soon. I love you.

Jalisa turns the paper over to see if there is more. She holds it up to the light in case there is some kind of secret message. She repeats it with the other letters as well. There is nothing more.

"Where's my husband, Tola?"

The question is rhetorical.

"Jesus, can you tell me?"

He doesn't.

"Tata wants us to leave, Mama," says Tola. "Immediately."

Jalisa takes a deep breath. "We're not leaving yet, Tola. Today we are going to rest. Your father said we could trust the Bukanis. We need to find my husband. We need answers and were going to start there."

They both join Lindi to draw and colour pictures. For a while it was like they were at home, waiting for Tata to come home. Tola looked toward the door now and then, half-expecting Tata to walk through the door.

Edna checks in on them around 1 pm. Jalisa insists on helping her prepare lunch which consists of umnqusho with beef and spinach. Mrs. Bukani has left for work so Jalisa decides to probe.

"How long have you worked for the Bukanis', Edna?"

"For about a year," says Edna. "Your husband made it easy for me to get used to the way they like things. I appreciated his assistance."

Jalisa smiles. "Are you married?"

"No, but I have a son in the village who lives with my mother. He's 15 years old and wants to be a pilot."

Jalisa sees that Edna is proud of her son. She glows as she speaks about him. As they converse, she finds it hard to imagine that Edna would do anything to jeopardize her son's future. But for many people, money talks. Her own husband was willing to do something out of character for a fee. She wasn't sure she could open up to Edna about what Thabo wrote in the letters.

She needn't have worried because Tola had no qualms about confronting her. He came barging into the kitchen.

"What have you done with my father?"

"Tola!" Jalisa is shocked at her son's behaviour.

Tola knew that his mom would disapprove but he didn't care. Something was amiss and he needed answers and beating around the bush would not achieve that end.

"We know that you are working for Mr. Wanjiru," Tola continues. "Tata was too or maybe he still is. We don't know. Please, what can you tell us?"

His voice cracks at the end which disarms the ladies. This journey is making a man of him too quickly, thinks Jalisa. She turns her gaze to Edna, letting silence demand a response.

"How do you know about Mr. Wanjiru?" asks Edna.

"Tata told us," blurts Tola before Jalisa can stop him. "Please answer my question."

"Tola, I don't know where your father is. Mr. Wanjiru approached me to spy on the Bukanis and I refused. I just wasn't comfortable doing that to my employer. Don't tell me that Thabo did."

They don't say anything.

"That surprises me. It goes against everything I know about him."

They don't say anything.

"What did Thabo find out?"

"He didn't find anything?" says Jalisa. "He felt that the Bukani's were good people and could be trusted. Do you believe that?"

"I do," says Edna. "They haven't given me any reason to believe otherwise."

Lindi comes running in. "Mama, Nomsa is crying."

"Go ahead," says Edna. "I'll plate the food and bring it in."

"I'll help you," says Tola.

When his mom and sister leaves, he apologizes.

"I'm really worried about my Tata," he explains. "What if something bad has happened to him?"

"Don't think that way, Tola. It's not useful and your family needs you to be positive. You said that you saw your Tata three weeks ago. Did he show any sign of stress?"

He didn't. He was his normal self. There was no reason to believe that something was amiss.

They bring lunch to the others. Edna joins them as well. After saying grace, Tola asks, "What can you tell us about Mr. Wanjiru?"

"Not much. After I refused to help him a couple of times, he didn't persist. I never saw him recruit Thabo and I have no idea if Cyril has been recruited. We don't talk much."

Jalisa finishes tending to Nomsa and joins them.

"You have a wonderful family, Jalisa. I'm sorry this harrowing experience has happened to them when they're so young."

"Thank you, Edna." Then she asks, "How did you get in touch with Mr. Wanjiru? Did he leave you a phone number?"

Edna shakes her head. "He said that he would be in touch with me. Why?"

"I want to find my husband, Edna. That's why."

Tola can't sleep. The whereabouts of his father weigh heavily on his mind. He pushes the blankets off, puts on his sneakers, and quietly slips outside. No one stirs.

It is a bright night. The cloudless sky exposes the uncountable number of stars and the moon lights up the heavens and the earth. That's why Tola can see Cyril talking with another man.

Curiosity getting the better of him, he sneaks forward. He doesn't recognize the man but the two of them are engaged in a heated conversation.

"What happened is not my fault," the man is saying. "That idiot wasn't careful. I warned him that these people are dangerous."

"Well, his family is here and they are asking questions," says Cyril. "Jalisa doesn't strike me as a woman who is going to leave here without some answers."

"I will leave that in your capable hands," says the man. "In the meantime, do you have any new information for me?"

"No, I don't."

"We don't feel like we're getting our money's worth, Cyril. Don't make us regret our investment."

"I think you guys are wrong, Mr. Wanjiru. The Bukanis are good people. You've got to tell me what I'm looking for."

"Good people? Tell that to Thabo. Do your job lest the same fate befalls you."

Tola listens to this exchange in horror. They were talking about Tata and it sounded like something bad had happened to him. He wishes that his mother was here because she would know what to do.

He decides to follow Mr. Wanjiru. He doesn't know why but it seems like a good idea. He wishes that he knew what time it was. He finds his way to Mr. Wanjiru's car which is unlocked, and settles into the back, behind the driver's side. He doesn't have to wait long.

Jalisa wakes up with a start. It must have been something she was dreaming about but she couldn't remember. She visits the bathroom and on her return, she looks at Nomsa and watches her sleep for a short while. Then she moves on to Lindi and smiles at how fast she's growing. Then she turns to look at her big man and notices the empty bed.

"Tola," she quietly calls out.

She steps outside and sees Cyril talking with a man. She also sees movement in the foreground and sees Tola creep toward the gate. *What is he doing?* She sees him climb into a car and as the man proceeds toward it, she walks quickly toward it. As the ignition brings the car to life and the car roars away, her hollers of Tola's name go unheeded.

"Who was that man?" she shrieks at Cyril, who wonders what is going on.

"What?"

"I saw Tola get into that car," Jalisa screams. "Where is he going?"

"Tola got into that car?" asks Cyril, understandably confused.

"Cyril, who is that man and where is that car going?"

Some lights come on in the community and a few doors open. Seeing Jalisa entangled with Cyril, the Bukani's approach the scene. Edna is with them.

"Jalisa, what is going on?" asks Mrs. Bukani.

"I saw Tola get into a car that belonged to a man Cyril was talking to. I need to know who it was and where they were going."

"Is that true, Cyril?" asks Mr. Bukani.

Cyril says nothing.

Jalisa slaps him. "Who is that man and where is my son going?"

Cyril breathes deeply. "That man's name is Mr. Wanjiru."

Jalisa gasps and looks at Edna.

"Jalisa, I have no idea where he is going," says Cyril.

"Who's Mr.Wanjiru?" asks Mr. Bukani.

No one said anything. Just Jalisa's sniffling broke the silence.

"Can we go inside sir," says Edna. "We have something we have to tell you."

As Edna and Cyril relay the story of Mr. Wanjiru, the Bukani's can't believe their ears. They say nothing except to gasp and to occasionally exclaim, "What?" Jalisa listens impatiently, occasionally speeding them up when she feels they are going off track with needless explanations.

"Where was Mr. Wanjiru taking my son?" she screams, panicking.

"I don't know, Jalisa," says Cyril. "I'm sorry."

Mr. Bukani speaks. "Can you get me the license plate of the car, Cyril?"

When Cyril brings it, he makes a phone call. He is heard talking to someone to let him know the owner of the car. It does come back with Mr. Wanjiru and he is given his address.

"Cyril, you're fired. Jalisa, I assume you want to come with me. My wife and Edna will look after your daughters. Let's go."

Tola shrinks to as small as he can as the car drives off. He wills his heart to stop thudding believing that Mr. Wanjiru will hear it. After a couple of minutes, he raises his head to see if he can see some landmark that will help him find his way back. He sees nothing. The light of the moon and stars is hindered by the clouds blanketing the night sky.

The trip isn't too long. Tola notices that it is another gated community and Mr. Wanjiru is let in by a female Cyril-type guard. Mr. Wanjiru drives into a garage and reaches to the back to retrieve his briefcase. It isn't until Mr. Wanjiru enters his house that Tola breathes again.

Believing the coast is clear, Tola steps out and peeks out of the garage. To his left is the gate with the guard reading a book. To his right is the quarters for all the domestics. It was a similar layout to the Bukani's community.

He steps lightly. He doesn't have to as everyone is still asleep but still. All curtains are drawn so he can't see inside any of the dwellings. He doubts that his Tata is in any of them but maybe someone knows something. He recalls the threat given to Cyril regarding the fate befallen his Tata.

He is just looking in the last window when two doors down, a lady comes screaming out with a wooden pestle lifted high. Tola responds with a scream of his own stopping her in her tracks.

She sees that he's just a boy. "Where is your mother? What are you doing looking in windows?"

Before Tola answers, other doors open, including one from the main house. Mr. Wanjiru strolls over inquiring what is going on as he approaches. The mini-crowd parts to show him.

"Who's this?"

It is all Tola can do to stop himself from grabbing the pestle and pounding this snake.

"My name is Tola Matthews, son of Thabo and Jalisa Matthews. What have you done with my Tata?"

It just comes out. Tola doesn't think about whether or not it is a good idea to reveal himself but it is done. Some eyes are on him while others are on Mr. Wanjiru. He stands there clearly stunned by the events.

He doesn't get a chance to respond as cars screech at the gate. Police demand that the gate opens and two cars enter, one a police car with two cops inside, and one other. They stop at Mr. Wanjiru's house and the crowd gets their attention.

"Tola!"

"Mama!"

They embrace as only a relieved mother and thankful son can. Mr. Bukani approaches with a couple of officers. They identify Mr. Wanjiru.

"Please, sir. Where is my husband?"

Mr. Wanjiru says nothing. He seems to be weighing his options.

"Am I under arrest?" he inquires.

"No, sir," replies Officer Kamau. "All we have now is a boy climbed into your car." He moved a step closer. "But that can change in a moment. Do you have an answer for the lady?"

"I want to speak to a lawyer," he informs the police.

The slap is a thunderclap. All the emotion of the journey from Dlambona to Lobani focussed on Jalisa's right hand and connects fully to Mr. Wanjiru's left cheek. He stumbles back against some of the domestic help.

"I want her charged with assault," he growls, clutching his cheek.

"What for?" asks Officer Kamau, who was the senior officer. "I didn't see anything."

Mr. Wanjiru looks around only to see everyone either shrug or begin to walk away.

"Speaking to a lawyer is your right," says Kamau. "But right now you're coming with us."

As they approach the cars, Jalisa looks at her son.

"You're going back to the Bukani's house with the officer. I will see you soon."

"Where are you going?" Tola asks, puzzled.

She answers by kissing his forehead and directing him to the police car. Tola is further confused when he sees Mr. Wanjiru going in Mr. Bukani's car instead of the police car.

"Mama, what is going on?"

Jalisa refuses to look at her little man. She climbs in the passenger side, with Mr. Bukani driving, and Kamau in the back with Mr. Wanjiru.

Tola watches them drive off in the opposite direction he was going, bewildered and worried.

Tola tries to stay awake. He wants to make sure that he sees his Tata when he walks in. Or he wants to be there for Mama should the worst be realized.

His eyes are heavy and fail him.

The white paint of a boy is washed off, and he is shined with sheep fat, anointing him as a man. Singing and dancing escort him back to the village, where others join in the celebration. Once he reaches his home, the fat is cleaned off and red clay applied to his face, marking his new status. Then he is given a seat of honour in the village square, and the celebration continued into the night.

The celebration is familiar to Tola. He has seen it many times in his village when boys are initiated into men by being circumcised. But he is twelve. It is done when a boy turns sixteen.

In the joyous crowd, is his Tata and Mama, singing loudly and looking at him proudly. Lindi comes running up to him and jumps up to hug him.

That awakens him and he tickles her to punish her as she had jumped on him in bed. She giggles with glee. He sees that there are others close, looking on. One is Mama with Nomsa in her arms.

The other is Tata.

"Hello, my son."

Epilogue

Tola never finds out how Jalisa was able to locate his Tata. He suspects that Mr. Wanjiru was encouraged to talk using means he didn't want to consider. He broaches the subject once with both his parents and is commanded not to do so again.

Tata is rehired by the Bukani's and the family stays there until they can depart for their home to survey the damages. Tata and Tola return to find not only their home destroyed, but the village decimated.

Though it is against the rules for families to stay in the servant's quarters, it is allowed for a month given the circumstances the Matthews' find themselves in. The Bukani's help to get Tola in the nearby Primary School for Grade 7.

Tata, Edna, and Cyril testify against Mr. Wanjiru. They never find out who he worked for and what the endgame was. He is not a government agent. He is more afraid of his bosses than of going to jail. He never goes to jail. One day he doesn't show up to court and he is never seen again.

Jalisa finds herself enjoying city living as Edna shows her around and introduces her to her circle of friends. Tata isn't sure he wants their children raised in the city. They decide to give it a year and then assess how things are going.

Tola is getting used to his new school. The class sizes are bigger, the teachers are meaner, and there is more work sent home.

He tries out for and makes the football team which makes the change more endurable.

Tata, Mama, Lindi, and Nomsa come to see his first game. His team wins 1- 0 and the family goes to get ice cream to celebrate. Ice cream is a new treat to the kids. They are enjoying it so much that they don't see a man watching them in a Peugeot 504 parked across the street.